A SWORDSMAN OF THE BRIGADE

A Swordsman
of the Brigade

by

MÍCHEÁL Ó hANNRACHÁIN

Abridged by
UNA MORRISSY

THE MERCIER PRESS
DUBLIN and CORK

The Mercier Press Limited
4 Bridge Street, Cork
25 Lower Abbey Street, Dublin 1

ISBN 0 85342 552 3

CONTENTS

ONE

One Night in Cathair Domnhaill

On a dark and stormy January night in 1703 Seamus Óg's stout little lugger crept stealthily out of a hidden creek on the Kerry coast and set her sails for France.

She was carrying young recruits for the famous Irish Brigade of the French army, among them myself, Piaras Grás, who had joined them that very night in flight from English soldiers.

I little thought the day before what was to befall me as I rode out to the fair of Cathair Domnhaill on my beautiful black mare, Crom. My father, old Seaghan Grás of Snaidhm Castle, had fought at Aughrim and lost his lands and his fortune to the victorious Williamites. But he managed to save a mare from the ruin of his fortune and bring her secretly to the little wayside cabin which was his home. Here her foal Crom was born and she became my best friend.

I had been busy all day at the fair, and on my way home I rode up to the inn kept by Mícheál Mór for I had some business to transact there. I completed it in a few minutes but as I came out and turned to mount my gentle Crom I felt a heavy hand on my shoulders. Looking round I saw Sir Michael Sickles, the William-ite supporter who had been given my father's lands and now lived in Snaidhm Castle, my former home.

'That's a fine mare,' he growled. 'I want a good mare just now and yours will suit me. I'll pay you the price

the law allows.' For well he knew that under the
Penal Laws he could take my splendid mare for just
£5 no matter what her real value.

At the very thought my fiery temper boiled over.
'You'll never own her,' I shouted furiously, and drawing a pistol I shot my beloved Crom dead.

Sir Michael, enraged, drew his sword and recklessly
I fired again. He fell, blood streaming from a wound
in his chest. As I stood horrified an arm dragged me
me back into the inn; Mícheál Mór, who had been a
servant of my father in the old days, had come to
my rescue. He rushed me to a room at the back with
a trap door leading to a cellar, and pulling up the
floor covering whispered to me to go down. As I
climbed down a ladder he closed the trap door and
replaced the covering.

Soon I heard the heavy tramp of soldiers and
voices questioning Mícheál, but at last they left. After
a time the door was raised and Mícheál called softly
to me to come out. Then he quickly took my own
coat and gave me a long cloak and a *caibin* to hide my
face.

'You daren't go home,' he said. 'They'll be watching. You'll have to leave the country. There's an
officer recruiting for the Brigade at An Curran. Go
over there and find Seamus Gabha. Tell him what
happened and that I sent you.' Then he shook my
hand and opened a door at the back. 'God watch over
you,' he whispered, and I left.

Moving with great caution and keeping to the fields
I reached An Curran at dawn and knocked at the old
forge. The black-bearded Seamus Gabha let me in

when I spoke Mícheál's name and I told him my story. Then he hid me in a recess under the fire-place and brought me food and drink.

I remained hidden all day but in the evening Seamus brought me out to meet a tall, broad-shouldered man who asked me if I wanted to join the Brigade.

'I do.'

'You're only just in time,' he said. 'Seamus Óg's boat sails tonight. We leave at once.'

I thanked Seamus Gabha for his kindness and we went out into the storm. After an hour we came to a creek and my companion whistled softly. A boat slid through the tossing waters and rowed us out to the lugger. All in one short day and night I had become a soldier of the Irish Brigade.

TWO

The Spy at 'Le Chat Rouge'

Three months after the stormy night when I had gazed at the receding shores of my native land I was wearing the uniform of Sheldon's Horse, and waiting to be send to tbe battlefields of the Rhine.

I was stationed in Dunkirk and one night some of us were in 'Le Chat Rouge' enjoying a glass of wine when a stranger entered dressed in the style of the Catalonian seamen with gold earrings and a red cap. He had long black hair and a thick beard. He called for wine and when Annette, the landlord's daughter, came to his table he tried to kiss her. She struggled and called to us for help. We jumped to our feet and I reached her first. I caught the stranger full in the face and his black beard fell off revealing a clean-shaven face, an English face.

Shouts of 'Spy' arose but as we closed on him he fired his pistol at the candelabrum and disappeared in the darkness. We rushed out and I almost caught up with him when he vanished around a corner. I turned to go back when I heard a step and then felt a stinging blow on the head.

*   *   *   *   *

When I came to I was lying on my back in the darkness, a bandage around my throbbing head. The place seemed to be swaying and I could not imagine where I was. Then the horrible thought came to me that I was aboard an English ship. They would take care not to let me escape for now I knew that there was an enemy ship in the French port. Even worse, I was an Irishman in the French army which was at war with them.

Footsteps came down the companion way and a lantern's gleam pierced the darkness. Two sailors pulled me to my feet and stood me before the Englishman of the inn, now in naval uniform.

'Who are you?' he demanded.

'Piaras Grás of Sheldon's Horse,' I replied proudly.

He began to question me about a Lieutenant O'Carroll of our regiment who had recovered plans stolen by an English spy.

'I won't tell you anything about him,' I said coolly.

'We'll see,' he said. 'Bo'sun, get your cat-o'-nine-tails,' he ordered.

As the bo'sun went, letting go of my right arm, I twisted free from the other sailor, tripped him and jumped on the officer. I sent him reeling and made for the companion way. Reaching the deck I tripped over a coil of rope and fell, which saved my life for something heavy whizzed just over my head.

I raced forward, leaped for the bulwarks and vaulted into the icy water. As I came to the surface I saw the beacon on the pier and, kicking off my heavy boots, I struck out desperately for the shore. I guessed they would not waste time pursuing me, nor fire a shot after me for that would alert the port authorities to their presence. At last I staggered ashore and fell senseless, and there the sentinels found me.

I recovered slowly and was once again in the saddle when news came that we were to join the army of the Rhine. Would I now see glory or share the fate of so many of my compatriots? Only the future would tell.

THREE

Speier—The Capture of the Standard

A cold, bright November moon shone on the smooth-flowing waters of the Rhine and on the tall cathedral of the ancient town of Speier which lay quiet beneath its shadow. It shone too on the rows of white tents and on the muskets and bayonets piled ready to be seized at dawn. From my lonely sentry post I could see the glow of our camp fires and hear the *Qui vive* of the other sentinels.

The word had gone out that tomorrow we would fight. During the day and well into the night our Commander-in-Chief, Marshal de Tallard, had inspected our forces, and now in the hours that were left before dawn the camp had become quiet and the soldiers had settled to snatch what rest they could before the shrill reveille would call them to battle.

All around me me slept and dreamed perhaps of home in Normandy or Brittany which they might never see again. My own thoughts roved back to my happy childhood spent in the woods and glens of Kerry; of the day my father rode out proudly at the head of a gallant array of armed men; of the black day of Aughrim, and of how it killed my mother; and how my father returned from Limerick a broken man.

*   *   *   *   *

The battle swayed to and fro as the Allies, commanded by the Prince of Hesse Cassel, rolled back our columns and even captured some of our guns. We of Sheldon's Horse were still held in reserve when an officer rode up to our colonel, Christopher Nugent of Dardistown, and gave him the order to charge. Our trumpets sounded and away we went like madmen, battle fever coursing through our veins. Steel clashed against steel, shouts and screams rose on the air. The tall form of a standard bearer galloped towards me; with a wild yell

I spurred toward him and we wrestled desperately for the trophy. A blow from my sabre sent him backwards off his horse and waving aloft the captured flag I galloped onwards. I remember little more of that day, but our charge paved the way for a French victory and led to the surrender of Landau which opened its gates to our troops three days after the victory of Speier.

Imagine my pride when the Marshal rode down our line drawn up after the battle and one of his staff officers beckoned me to him. When I rode forward with the captured flag waving proudly over my head the Marshal asked me my name.

'Piaras Grás of Sheldon's Horse,' I told him.

'Ah! *Un Irlandais brave*,' he said.

Some days later I was summoned to our colonel's tent. He praised me for my action, and informed me that I had been named ensign of my regiment.

'Try to do as well in the future and promotion awaits you,' he told me.

'A Grás always does his best, *Mon Colonel*,' I replied.

FOUR

The Mountain Inn

One stormy night on a lonely mountain road near the Italian border I reined in my weary horse before a darkened inn where I hoped to find food and shelter for the night. After repeated knockings a surly land-lord at last thrust his head out of a window and growled hoarsely, 'What do you want at such an hour?'

'Food and lodging for myself and stabling for my horse,' I called to him.

With much muttering and grumbling and a great rattling of bolts and locks he finally opened the door and invited me in.

'But my horse, landlord,' I said.

'I'll see to him presently,' he replied.

'No,' I said. 'My horse is my care. I will stable him myself.'

Cursing under his breath he led me round to a ramshackle shed where I did the best I could to make my horse comfortable. Then I went inside. He poked up the fire and set out an unappetising meal of cold meat and black bread, with a flagon of wine. I was hungry enough to eat anything and the wine turned out to be good.

I thought he might have some information which would be useful to me, so I tried some talk but he rebuffed every attempt. I decided on another approach, so I lit a cigar and puffed the pleasant fragrance across the room. His eyes glistened greedily and I politely asked if he would have one. He took it eagerly and soon was smoking with the enjoyment of a man who seldom saw a Spanish cigar.

'That is good wine of yours,' I said, trying again.

'You will pardon the rough food,' he said, the cigar having put him in better humour. 'A troop of German soldiers was here earlier and ate up everything. They were looking for a Frenchman carrying despatches. They left about an hour before you came.'

He stopped suddenly as if he had said too much, and I did not want to arouse his suspicions by appearing too curious. Just then his wife came in to say my room was ready. But he had told me enough. The road was watched and I was storm-bound in the inn. I thought of going on but I knew I could miss my footing in the wild night and crash to my death down the mountain pass.

So I went upstairs and threw my boots off noisily as though undressing. Then I blew out the candle and sat down on the bed to think. Here was I, Lieutenant Piaras Grás of Sheldon's Horse, with important despatches for the Duc de Vendôme who was engaged in the siege of Ivrea across the Italian border. The enemy were on my track and I could not trust the landlord.

Just then I heard stealthy footsteps. Stretching out on the bed I began to snore loudly. The steps moved on, as though the listener were reassured by my snores, and after a few minutes I heard the opening and shutting of a door. Creeping to the window, which was barred, I looked out into the stormy blackness when a flash of lightning showed me a figure slouching away.

I guessed it was my landlord gone to find the Germans who had undoubtedly promised him a handsome reward for catching the Frenchman. I tried the door. It was locked and I realised that I was trapped. Keeping cool I relit the candle and searched the room; then I hid the despatches where the landlord would never find them, primed my two pistols and lay down. A good sleep would sharpen my wits, and there was nothing more I could do tonight.

FIVE

Betrayed

The sun was streaming into the room when I awoke and the night's fierce storm had passed. I dressed quickly, tried the door and found it unlocked. Doubtless the landlord would be hoping that I had guessed nothing.

As I went down the stairs I heard the clinking of glasses and the sound of a German drinking song, so the landlord's midnight journey had not been in vain. I entered the dining room and met the eyes of half a dozen German dragoons. I bade the company good morning and sat down near the fire where I could have a better view of them. There was no doubt that I was suspect, so I decided that I had better play the thing boldly.

Calling for breakfast I urged the landlord to hurry for I wanted to get on the road again as quickly as possible. 'And bring me a couple of bottles of your best wine,' I added. 'Some of these gentlemen might care to drink with me.'

The proposal was greeted with shouts of approval, and when he had set the wine before me I called a toast as I filled their glasses. 'Here's to Prince Eugene,'

I cried, 'and confusion to the French.' They drank
heartily to that, and when the landlord set breakfast
before me they gathered around the table and asked
many questions as to where I was going and what
service I had seen which were not easy to answer. I
hinted darkly at some very secret work on behalf of
the Emperor and then, having finished, I rose and
ordered the landlord to bring round my horse.

As I made to leave a sergeant stepped up to me and
saluting stiffly said, 'I am sorry, sir, but you cannot
leave for the moment. We know that a Frenchman is
due to come this way with despatches and we have
orders to search everyone.'

I protested that as an emisssary of the Emperor I
should not have to submit but he remained firm, so I
decided that it would be wiser to give in. I threw
them my boots which they examined carefully, then
each article of my clothing, but they could glean
nothing from them. I had taken care of that. Some-
what nonplussed they let me go, the sergeant saluting
as I rode away.

The wild beauty of the mountain scenery and the
music of the foaming torrents as they hurtled down
the gorge would have delighted me on another
occasion. Now, however, I could think of nothing but
the safety of my despatches. I had pledged my word
to carry them speedily to Ivrea. My honour and my
whole career were at stake. I believed that the soldiers
would stick to the letter of their instructions and
search only the people they encountered. I did not
think that they would search my room.

I rode for long enough to give them time to depart

and then I turned my horse's head and retraced the
road that I had come.

SIX

Fooled—I win Through

Several hours had passed when I rode up to the inn
again. The dragoons had gone and I told the landlord
that I had lost a valuable ring and wished to search
my room for it.

I retrieved the despatches but had reckoned without
him. As I turned to leave the room he was standing in
the doorway grinning. I sprang towards him but he
slammed the door, pushing the bolt into place.

'Now my clever soldier,' he shouted, 'you can cool
your heels until the Germans come back.'

Furious with myself for allowing the wretch to
outwit me I ran to the barred window only to see him
galloping off on my own horse. His impudence made
me laugh in spite of my predicament, but then I gave
my mind to the serious task of seeing how I might
defend myself and my precious despatches.

The door was solid and I pulled the heavy table
against it. Then I piled other furniture against that
and waited. In about half an hour I heard the jingle of
a troop and looking out saw about twenty dragoons
with a tall officer at their head. The landlord, looking
well satisfied with himself, was riding beside the
sergeant who had insisted on searching me.

Heavy footsteps pounded up the stairs and angry voices ordered me to give up the despatches while blows rained on the door. Then a different sound caught my ear and turning swiftly I was just in time to see a dragoon, mounted on a ladder, aiming his musket at me. Rushing across I drove my sword through his arm and wrenching a piece of timber from the bed I pushed the ladder away from the window. As it crashed with its burden I saw it break in two.

Meanwhile the attack on the door continued and at last the upper half gave way and the faces of the dragoons showed through the opening. My position behind the barricade helped me and I fought through the gap wounding several men. I was not the most noted swordsman in Sheldon's for nothing. But numbers were against me and I could not hold out for ever.

Suddenly an order rang out and fighting stopped. The tall officer I had seen riding at the head of the troop stepped forward.

'This is a lengthy business,' he said. 'We could settle it man to man. I am noted for my fencing; so apparently are you. If I defeat you you will give me your despatches.'

'And if I refuse?' I asked.

'In that case,' he said grimly, 'the musketeers. . .'

What right had I to place the Duc's despatches at the hazard of a personal fight? Yet what other choice had I?

'Very well,' I agreed, 'but first, with your permission, I will smoke a cigar. May I offer you one?'

He accepted and I had gained the respite I badly needed. As we smoked we talked of our boyhoods, his in Silesia, mine in green Eire. Then time was up and we ranged against one another, the dragoons stacking their arms to watch.

Though he fought skilfully I had the advantage. He was taller but I was lighter and faster. Gradually I edged towards the door and finally, with a swift lunge, I broke his guard and ran him through the chest.

In a bound I was through the doorway and down the stairs. I rushed for the open where my horse was still standing. As I leapt on his back I heard shots and felt a searing pain in my left arm, but I spurred my horse and went flying down the road. Dragoons mounted and followed but we sped away in the dusk.

Later that night, my left arm useless but my despatches safe, I stood before the Duc and delivered them, soiled and stained with blood.

'M. de Grás,' he said, 'you have done wonders.'

'Milord Maréchal,' I replied, 'I had pledged my word.'

SEVEN

In Hospital—A Memory of the Homeland

The wound in my arm and consequent loss of blood brought on an attack of fever which kept me in bed in the military hospital for several weeks. There I met many soldiers of Dillon's Regiment and we spent much of our time together, passing the weary hours playing cards and smoking.

I became particularly friendly with one officer, Lieutenant Muiris Ó Briain, a grey-haired veteran of many campaigns. We seemed to be drawn together and I remembered that I had heard my father speak of a Muiris Ó Briain, though I knew nothing of how they had been connected.

One day when most of the others had resumed duty we were sitting alone, smoking and chatting of the old country and he asked me my father's Christian name.

'Seaghan,' I told him. 'Seaghan Grás of Snaidhm. He served from the Boyne to Aughrim and defended Limerick. After it had fallen he came back to Snaidhm, but he did not enjoy his old home for long.'

'Is he dead?'

'He died of a broken heart, and I am here in France, the last of the Gráses.'

'Then I knew him well,' said Ó Briain. 'He saved my life after Aughrim. But do not grieve for him. At least he is at rest and at home. He is better off than I am. I will never see my home again.'

'Why not? Our fortunes might change,' said I with all the enthusiasm of youth. But he shook his head sadly.

'No,' he said. 'My heart tells me that I will never again gaze on the wild Atlantic from the top of Moher. Wife, country, friends — all are gone.'

'Tell me about yourself,' I urged him. 'My father often spoke about you.'

'Yes,' he said warmly, 'he remembered. Well, my

story is brief enough. It is like many another which could be related by our comrades-in-arms.'

EIGHT

Ó Briain's Story

'I will begin by saying that I was the happiest man in Clare when King James landed in Kinsale in March of '89. I was young, light-hearted and just married to a beautiful girl. When news of the war came she urged me to join the defenders of our land, and so I marched away one bright morning with a gallant company. We fought by the Boyne after King James had fled, and we campaigned long and bitterly, often hungry, barefoot and ragged.

'Then came the black day of Aughrim. I had met your father previously and we became close friends. On that day we fought side by side and when, after our general was killed, the tide of battle turned against us, I was badly wounded. Your father brought me from the field of battle and he and some of his men took me the long, painful journey home. Then having left me safely with Máire they turned back to Limerick. I never saw him again.'

I remained silent, thinking of my father, and he went on: 'Máire nursed me back to health and for a while we were left alone in our wild Atlantic home. My little piece of land was poor enough but it aroused the envy of a neighbour, one Trasker. I was on the list

of outlaws who had fought the Williamites, and when
Trasker reported it my land was forfeit. We took
refuge in a mountain shieling and I was happy enough
for I had Máire.

'But the black Trasker learned of it and one day,
when I was away from the house, he came with
soldiers to take me. Máire told him I was not there,
and then he tried to put his arms around her. Enraged
because she resisted him and alarmed at her screams,
he emptied his pistol into her breast and rode off.

'What a sight met my eyes when I returned shortly
after! Just inside the door lay Máire in a pool of
blood, still breathing but her life ebbing fast. When I
asked her what had happened she gasped the name of
Trasker and begged me to leave the country at once.
Not long afterwards she passed peacefully away in my
arms. I think I went mad then.

'All that possessed me was the thought of revenge.
I roamed the countryside searching for Trasker. I
could not get to him at home for his house was
guarded. Then one night I saw him, riding along a
road which runs by the cliffs. I sprang out from the
shadows and cried to him to halt. He tried to draw a
pistol but I dragged him from his horse. In my mad-
ness I had the strength of a dozen men.

' "Who are you?" he demanded.

' "Muiris Ó Briain, whose wife you murdered."

'He tried to bargain with me then.

' "I will give you back your land," he pleaded
hoarsely.

' "Can you give me back my murdered wife?" I
shouted.

'Suddenly he drew his pistol but the shot missed me and he turned and fled. As he reached the cliff I fired, and with a wild yell he leaped and went crashing to the beach far below.

'I hid among the people until the hue and cry died down and then I crossed to France. I have fought in many campaigns since then, but one day soon my life will go out in the hurly-burly of a charge and the spirit of Muiris Ó Briain will be at rest.'

We were silent for a while, and then he spoke again. 'If ever you need a friend,' he said, 'call on me. I owe that to your father.'

I shook his hand in gratitude, little knowing how soon I would gladly remember those words.

NINE

A Girl's Appeal

My arm improved and I looked forward to rejoining my regiment. My spirits began to rise at the prospect but I had reckoned without fate. Instead I received orders from the Duc de Vendôme seconding me for the time being to Dillon's Regiment and attaching me to his personal staff. Apparently he had been impressed by my handling of the despatches and decided to make me an aide-de-camp. I was deeply disappointed, and would have greatly preferred my own regiment.

One day he gave me a letter to deliver to M. le

Chevalier de Frobin, Colonel of the Regiment of Béarn. This man, who had the reputation of being a brave soldier but something of a *roué*, was quartered in an imposing house, and I was shown into an elegant room to await him. As I gazed around at its luxurious furnishings I was astonished to see a curtain part and a girl peep through with her finger on her lips. She was tall, of a dark Italian type of beauty, with great black eyes in which were blended hope and fear. She could not have been more than twenty.

She came swiftly towards me and whispered, 'I am a prisoner of de Frobin. Will you help me?'

'If I can, mademoiselle,' I replied, wondering what all this could mean.

A footstep sounded in the hall and she said hastily, 'The Chevalier must not know that I spoke to you. Come to the green door by the grove at nine tonight. Tell no one.' Then she glided away behind the curtain as the Chevalier came in. He read the letter, gave me a message and I returned to camp.

Since she had pledged me to silence I could not confide in Ó Briain and I pondered at length on the girl's strange appeal. Was it a trap, designed by someone aggrieved at my staff-appointment to entangle me with the Chevalier, and so with the Duc who was a personal friend of his? Was she mad? I decided that I would at least listen to her story.

Accordingly I was standing at the green door at nine when a hand touched mine in the darkness and a voice said softly, 'Thank you for your trust.'

'How can I help you,' I asked.

'I am the daughter of the Vaudois chief, Henri

Neffer,' she told me. 'I am a hostage here. Can you
help me to escape? I feel that you are a gentleman
and understand my position in the hands of this man.'

Indeed I sympathised, but what could I do? To
appeal to the Duc would be useless. He would only be
amused by his friend's gallantries towards his charming hostage. Besides, her father was a guerrilla leader
who had often attacked French supplies. Yet the girl
was in a desperate situation.

'Supposing I could get you through our lines,
where would you go?'

'A shepherd who lives in the mountains three hours'
ride from here would hide me and tell my father.'

I had been thinking that with Ó Briain's help we
could disguise her and take her through the passes
one dark night. But how to get the disguise to her?

'That lighted window is my room,' she said. 'There
is thick, strong ivy outside. Could you climb up and
bring it to me?'

It seemed a desperate venture, but what else
offered?

'I will come tomorrow night,' I whispered. 'Keep a
light in the window and be careful not to rouse
suspicion.'

A woman's voice called her and she turned back
into the garden.

'Farewell and thank you, my generous friend,' she
said and slipped away.

I galloped back to camp, filled with whirling
thoughts.

TEN

The Escape

Muirís Ó Briain willingly agreed to help me when I told him in what danger the girl stood, though he warned me of the likely consequences if the Chevalier should ever hear of it.

We ascertained that he would, in fact, be out on special duty that night, and we secured an officer's uniform for Mademoiselle Neffer. Muirís was to see to the horses; I would deliver the disguise.

The night fell black and threatening which suited our purpose, and about an hour after dark we rode up to a clump of trees where Muirís would wait. I stole forward and made my way through the garden. I climbed the ivy under the lighted window and tapped. The light went out and Aimée Neffer's face appeared. I handed her the bundle which I had tied to my belt and whispered to her to make haste. At the foot of the ivied wall I waited, and soon I heard a rustle and she stood beside me.

'Come then,' I said, 'Ó Briain is waiting with the horses.'

She was startled to hear of another officer, but I reassured her that she could trust him. 'Without his help I would have been unable to help you,' I told her.

We joined him and rode away into the darkness. It was raining hard now and it was unlikely that we would meet anyone except soldiers on duty. Fortun-

27

ately the area was guarded by an outpost of Dillon's and I had made sure to find out the password. I warned Aimée to keep silent whatever happened and hardly had I done so when we heard the sound of men coming towards us. When the challenge came I answered and was stunned to hear the voice of the Chevalier saying, 'Ah, you are riding late, Lieutenant Grás.'

I answered with some laughing comment on the bad weather and we rode on, but Ó Briain muttered to me as we spurred away, *'M'anam,* what ill wind drove the Chevalier in our direction tonight?'

We did not approach the pass where Dillon's held guard but, guided by Aimée, turned on to a rocky defile which would take us outside the French lines. We had to lead our horses over some rough ground and the going was difficult. We had toiled for a few hours deeper into the mountains when Aimée suddenly said, 'Gaspard's cottage is just ahead.'

I followed the direction of her finger but could see nothing. She led on unerringly and soon we stood before a cottage in a little clearing. She knocked and uttered a peculiar cry, and the door was opened by a tall, bearded man carrying a musket. He was overjoyed to see her but would have shot us forthwith had she not told him of our help in her escape.

'We part here, my brave friends,' said Aimée Neffer. 'How can I ever thank you for all you have done? But I shall never forget you and perhaps in the future I may be able to pay back a little of my debt.'

The gallant Muiris raised her hand to his lips. 'May you never again need a friend, *a chailín dubh dílís,*' he said, and turned to follow Gaspard who was to guide us down the mountain.

Aimée caught my hand in both of hers and I heard her sob. Then she turned and fled into the cottage. Surprised, I waited for a moment but she did not reappear; then I turned to follow the others. I looked back after I had gone a little distance and I fancied I could see her standing gazing after us.

We followed the silent Gaspard until our watch fires could be seen twinkling afar off on the plain. Then with a very curt 'good night' he turned back and alone we made our way back to camp.

ELEVEN

The Whipping of the Chevalier

A couple of weeks passed by swiftly. The Duc was pushing forward in his campaign and my increased duties had almost put the midnight adventure out of my mind. I had met the Chevalier once or twice, but he had given no sign that he suspected me of helping his prisoner to escape.

Then one night the episode was brought back to me with staggering suddenness. A number of us were playing cards in a ruined house out of range of fire when the Chevalier swaggered in. He came over to where I was and asked if I were as successful in cards as in playing the gallant. I made no reply but my partner protested indignantly at the interruption.

'I have an affair to settle with this gentleman,' said the Chevalier.

'Then settle it outside,' said my partner.

'This is the place to settle it,' he replied, 'where all can hear.'

I had still said nothing and my silence appeared to enrage him. Raising his voice so that everyone could hear he said, 'if this young man were of equal rank I would force him to fight. Since he is not, I will chastise him.' He produced a whip.

I stood up and placing a chair between him and myself asked calmly, 'of what do you accuse me?'

'How unfortunate for you,' he said, 'that I met you with your mountain wench that night. You are not fit to wear the King's uniform.'

'If you hold it a crime to help a lady escape from a house where she is held for vile purposes by the noble gentleman who owns it, then I will confess to it,' I replied.

Furiously he kicked aside the chair and made a rush at me and we struggled but I wrenched the whip from his hands.

'Now, Monsieur,' I gritted, 'you will apologise for your insults to the lady.'

'Never,' he shouted.

'Monsieur,' I cried, 'you wanted publicity to chastise me. Now you shall have it for your own chastisement.'

My partner laid a hand on my arm. 'De Grás,' he said, 'the affair has gone far enough. You will ruin yourself.'

I shook off his hand. I was in a white heat of passion

by now and would, I believe, have ignored my commanding officer, the Duc himself. Curling the whip in the air I brought it down around the Chevalier's shoulders while I held him as in a vice. He struggled and cursed but I kept on until my arm ached. Then I flung him down, where he lay for a few seconds, and breaking the whip into a couple of pieces I flung it at him.

'*M'anam*,' I cried, 'you know now what it is to insult a lady. She fortunately is beyond your power. But if your rank does not preclude you from seeking revenge on me I will give you satisfaction.'

With the look of a fiend he got to his feet.

'You have won this time, De Grás,' he snarled, 'but we will meet again.'

He strode out amid the hush which had fallen on the room and Ó Briain who had come in during the fracas walked across to me.

'This is unfortunate, Piaras,' he said. 'He will try to harm you. But if he challenges you, allow me to act for you.'

I gripped his hand. Since we all knew that the Duc strictly forbade duelling among his officers during a campaign I was beginning to understand just what Muiris Ó Briain's friendship really meant.

TWELVE

The Challenge—The Duel—The Arrest

The following morning two officers came to my
quarters. One of them, the Comte de Bellerive,
presented me with the Chevalier's terms. He had
been grossly and publicly insulted, he said, but did
not wish to be harsh with one who perhaps did not
understand the code governing such matters. He
would not, therefore, enforce his right of compelling
me to fight if I would agree to make a public apology
to him in the presence of the same people before
whom I had insulted him.

'And if I refuse?' I asked.

'Then he would require you to fight,' said the
Comte, 'though as a nobleman he is not obliged to
fight with someone of lesser rank.'

'Gentlemen,' I replied, 'I accept the duel. My
friend, Lieutenant Muiris Ó Briain, will discuss details
with you. Adieu.'

At that they bowed and left. Had they really
thought, I wondered, that I would apologise to this
man to save him from fighting an inferior? They did
not know Piaras Grás.

In the evening Ó Briain came to tell me that the
meeting was to be in the morning, the weapons
swords.

'He is a fine swordsman,' warned Muiris, 'but then
you know something about swordplay yourself.'

32

I tried to banish disturbing thoughts. The combat did not worry me but the Duc's anger did. Duelling was forbidden. In addition, if these other thought so much about rank, how much more might be, a duke of France. It was in his power to ruin me if he wished. And if I had foreseen the other consequences which were to follow from the unfortunate affair I almost think I would have apologised.

* * * * *

In the cold grey dawn we faced each other. The Comte de Bellerive came across to me. His principal, he said, wished to give me another chance to withdraw. He did not wish to ruin me and urged me to think of the Duc's anger. I became angry then and Muiris, seeing the Comte speaking to me, hurried forward.

'Monsieur,' he remonstrated, 'the time for that is past. I am surprised at you.'

The word was given then and our weapons crossed with a hiss which well expressed the Chevalier's hatred of me. I was pondering on his action in sending the Comte to speak when the point of his sword grazed my shoulder.

'*Seachain. Seachain, a mhic*,' exclaimed Muiris. 'Think only of the duel.'

Then I realised that the Chevalier's motive had been to distract me and I had fallen into his trap. I gave my whole energy to the fight then, and with a lightning twist of my wrist sent my opponent's weapon clattering away.

'Strike,' he shouted hoarsely, as I dropped the point of my sword. 'Strike.' But I made no move.

'My principal is satisfied,' said Ó Briain, for he knew that I had no desire to kill the Chevalier.

The nobleman's eyes blazed. 'I accept no favours from him,' he rasped. 'The fight goes on.'

We returned to the combat, feinting and parrying, and suddenly I found an opening in his guard. As my sword hung poised we heard the sound of galloping horses and the Chevalier swerved slightly. My sword entered his body at a vital point and he fell.

The horses approached and a voice cried, 'What is this?' Towering over us was the Duc de Vendôme.

'Speak, some of you,' he thundered.

'Milord,' stammered the Comte, 'the Chevalier challenged this gentleman and. . .'

'And I have lost one of my best officers,' finished the Duc in a fury. 'You will all report to my quarters. Lieutenant de Grás, you are under arrest.'

He turned and rode away, and as I rode behind him I wondered what Aimée Neffer would say to the tragic outcome of our adventure.

THIRTEEN

The Duc's Alternative

I had been confined to prison for a week and was beginning to feel deeply despondent. I did not fear death, if such were the Duc's decision, nor was my conscience troubled about the Chevalier's death. I deeply regretted it, but it had been an accident. I would have given much if the whole affair had never happened at all, but the past is dead and we cannot recall it. It was the monotony and uncertainty which weighed on me. To be cut off from friends, to have nothing to do but brood made the hours seem like days and the days like weeks.

Then one morning a military escort was sent to bring me to the Duc's quarters. When I entered he signalled to the others to leave and sat for some time looking at me in silence.

At last he said, 'I was just considering if I would have you shot.' After a pause he continued, 'you have been responsible for the death of one of my best officers and best friends.'

'No one regrets it more than I, Milord,' I said, 'but the fight was forced upon me.'

'How?' he asked.

I told him the story, omitting only Aimée Neffer's name, and when I had finished he said, 'I have known something of the story for some time, so it is well you did not try to lie to me or I would have had you before the firing squad within the hour. Nevertheless your life is forfeit. You are too brave and too clever a man to shoot out of hand or send to prison for life. I will give you a chance for your life; you may accept or reject it.

'Up in the mountains between Briançon and Susa,' he said, pointing to a map spread before him, 'the Sieur de la Genèvre, a former ally, has gone over to our enemy, the Duke of Savoy. His castle, which is almost impregnable, commands a pass and he has done much damage to our convoys. It would take an army to defeat him, and I have neither the men nor the time. But one or two men could carry out the plan I have in mind. I want the Sieur brought here as a hostage for the good behaviour of his followers.

'I am not interested in how this is done. All that matters to me is the capture of the Sieur de la Genèvre. If you can accomplish this your life and military rank will be restored. If you fail, the Sieur will hardly allow you to escape.

'Now, which is it to be? The firing squad here or a chance to serve the King and win back your rank?'

I thought it over for a while. Death threatened me from both sides but whereas here it was close, in the mountains it was a little more remote.

'Milord,' I said. 'I accept the chance.'

'Bravo,' said the Duc.

'I may bring a friend with me?'

'Yes, yes. Make your own arrangements,' he said rising.

Saluting I turned on my heel and went out to attempt the near impossible.

FOURTEEN

In the Mountains

And so within a few days Muiris and I were to be found making our way with difficulty up a steep mountain pass over which we had been travelling for hours. Above us in the clear mountain air we could catch glimpses of the pointed roofs of the little village where our journey would end, perhaps for ever. In the background, towering over the houses, could be seen the battlements of the Sieur's castle. A flag fluttered from one of its turrets.

As we guided our horses over the rough road a tall, bearded man emerged from the pine forest which bordered the mountainous way. He carried a musket and a well-filled game bag and he saluted us as we passed. We returned his greeting and I asked him if we could find lodgings in the village.

'We seldom have strangers,' said the mountaineer looking curiously at us, 'but you will probably find what you want at *Le Coq Doré*.'

We had decided that I should pose as a visitor from Turin come to sample the hunting in the mountains and Muiris as my serving man. But it was clear from what the mountainer said that we would be looked upon with suspicion in this remote place whoever we were, especially if we were obliged to stay any length of time. However we rode on to *Le Coq Doré* and ordered a meal and accommodation.

The inn was tiny and the landlord apologetically explained to us that we would have to share a bedroom. I pretended to be put out by this but it was actually a stroke of good fortune for now Muiris and I could make our plans more easily.

We rose early each morning and went out into the mountains to hunt. We had decided to keep away from the village as much as possible to avoid making the inhabitants inquisitive, and we hoped too that in the mountain passes we might stumble on information which could be of use to us. But though we shot plenty of game for the next two weeks we could learn nothing of the Sieur, nor of how we might approach his stronghold.

Then one day a strange thing happened. We were tracking a chamois along a path which would bring us closer than we had ever been to the château when we heard a shot and looked up to see a man above us on a rock with his musket trained on us.

'Halt,' he called. 'The Sieur does not like strangers too close to his château.'

'Why not?' I demanded.

'That's not for me to say,' he replied. 'But he does not welcome strangers here or in his village.'

It was clear from this, as we had feared all along, that the Sieur was fully informed about our sojourn in his village and was warning us to leave.

When we returned to *Le Coq Doré* a note awaited us addressed to M. de Berac which was the name I was using as the visitor from Turin. It was from the Sieur himself advising us that the mountain passes were not good for hunting; that the roads around the château were very dangerous; and wishing us a pleasant journey back to Turin.

'The turn of the game has come,' said Muiris. 'I wonder what his next move will be.'

We were soon to know.

FIFTEEN

The Sieur Strikes

We stayed on at *Le Coq Doré* and for four days heard nothing more from the man we now knew to be our enemy. We made no change in our behaviour other than to keep our pistols primed and our swords ready, but the landlord changed his significantly. He served our meals late or badly cooked; he gave us bad wine; he spilt food and splashed soup on my clothes. Then one day he came out into the open and said, 'no doubt you will be leaving soon. You have seen enough of our mountains.'

'There are many interesting things yet to be seen,' I replied. 'The château for instance would repay a visit I'm sure.'

'The château is not for inspection,' he said sharply, 'and our mountains can be very dangerous. Many accidents have happened.'

Clearly he was trying to frighten us off. However we acted as usual, going out and saying we would be back at dusk for dinner. When we returned in the evening we found the inn filled with a noisy rabble of well-armed fellows. We pushed our way through them to the dining room but there was no sign of dinner. Calling for the landlord we demanded our meal.

He told us sullenly, 'you cannot dine here tonight.'

'Why not?' I demanded.

'I have had my orders,' he replied, starting to back

39

out of the room. Some of the riff-raff from outside were peering in and my temper began to rise.

'You need a lesson,' I began, moving towards him, but he caught a heavy tankard from the table and hurled it at my head. As if on a signal the rabble pushed their way into the room shouting, 'Out with the spy' and Muiris, who had been watching silently, drew his sword and sprang to my side.

They came at us then but they were not skilled and our swift thrusts drove a couple of them back howling. Still, they greatly outnumbered us and we were hard pressed enough. Using the big table as a barrier we pushed it towards them crushing them closer and keeping them at bay at either end of it. Suddenly the men in front drew back and fell silent. In the lull I heard a slight sound behind and yelling to Muiris, 'Guard the front' I turned to see two men coming through a door at the back of the room.

One of them was the bearded mountaineer we had met on our first day. The other rushed forward, stumbled, and the point of my sword went through his shoulder. The mountaineer lifted his musket and swung it above his head to brain me. I leaped aside but the musket butt snapped off my sword at the hilt. I sprang at him as he swayed with the blow and we grappled; then with a sudden twist I had learned in Kerry I tossed him on his back, his head crashing against the floor.

Turning back to Muiris I saw that the fight was nearly over. The mob, disheartened by the failure of the rear attack, had turned and fled through the other door.

We called for some good wine to restore us and the
landlord brought it in looking frightened and muttering that the Sieur was a dangerous man to cross. I
insisted he have a glass with us, and then Muiris and I
helped him to clear the debris from the room. We
revived the unconscious mountaineer with some wine
and sent him on his way.

Then at long last we sat down to our delayed
dinner.

SIXTEEN

An Unlooked-for Friend

Now that we had a little time to think I saw the
gravity of our situation. The Sieur might not strike
again that night but we would have to move to
different quarters in the morning. Just then a pleasant
girlish voice broke in on my sombre thoughts. Some
traveller had arrived and we heard the landlord
greeting her. Muiris and I looked at one another.

'That voice sounds familiar,' I said.

'I'd wager a year's pay that it is the voice of Mademoiselle Aimée Neffer,' said Muiris.

The landlord threw open the door and ushered in a
charming young lady dressed in a becoming riding
habit and a jaunty hat with white plumes. Apologising
for the smallness of his inn he asked if she would
object to the presence of two gentlemen. We rose and
I asked if she would dine with us. As she turned

haughtily towards me I said, 'Mademoiselle Neffer, do you not remember?'

With a cry of delight she said, 'Monsieur de Grás! Who would have expected to meet you here.' Then turning to the landlord she said, 'I will dine with these gentlemen. They are my friends.'

After some pleasant talk she asked what we were doing in this place since the Sieur was no friend of the French. I could not tell her the whole unhappy story; it would upset her deeply to be the cause of our desperate adventure and it would not help us.

'Do not ask, Mademoiselle,' I said. 'The Sieur is a friend of yours.'

'He is no friend of mine,' she said hotly. 'He is an ally of my father. But I feel that something is wrong. Please tell me. I may be able to help you.'

'We cannot bring you into this, Mademoiselle,' I told her.

She reminded me indignantly that she had the right to repay a debt. 'What has happened?' she continued. 'Has your aiding me made the Chevalier your enemy?'

'The Chevalier is dead,' I said unthinkingly, revealing the very thing I had intended to keep from her.

'Dead,' she cried. 'He fell by your hand. I see it all now.'

I could have bitten my tongue out for my foolish slip, but I had to tell her the whole story now, if only to show her that she was blameless in the matter.

She listened in silence and then said quietly, 'my debt to you is much greater than I had thought. Can you forgive me for being the cause of bringing you on this dangerous quest?'

'To have saved you from that villain counts for more with me than all the danger,' I told her, 'but you can see why I cannot accept your help. It would compromise you with your father's ally. All I can ask of you is silence. Even in that there may be treachery to your people.'

'If so I will do that treachery,' Aimée replied. 'But be careful. Danger is all around you. And if we do not meet again, remember that Aimée Neffer may yet pay her debt.'

'Mademoiselle, you may yet get that opportunity,' I said.

After she had retired Muiris wondered if I had been wise to reveal our mission to her. 'Remember,' he said, 'she is one of these mountaineers herself.'

'Muiris,' I said, 'I would trust that girl with my life. But in any case the Sieur is as much our enemy now as if he knew why we are here.'

And so we went to bed, but with our arms at the ready and one on watch while the other slept, in case the Sieur should strike during the night.

SEVENTEEN

Prisoners—Disillusion

How much time had passed I do not know, only that a pale dawn was breaking when I was awakened by the crash of the door being forced in. It had been my watch and I had failed. I had paced the floor and smoked a pipe to keep awake, but exhaustion had overtaken both my will power and my soldier's training and now disaster had struck.

I shouted a warning to Muiris and snatched up a pistol, but too late. It was knocked out of my hand and three or four men jumped on me. Within minutes our struggle was over and Muiris and I were lying tightly bound, prisoners of the Sieur de la Genèvre.

There was a noise outside and he came in to inspect us accompanied by the landlord carrying candles. He was a short, stoutly built man with a scraggy, tawny-coloured beard, not what I had expected from his redoubtable reputation. He asked the landlord if he had discovered anything further about us and to my horror the landlord produced a paper which he told the Sieur he had found in my pocket. It was the letter from the Duc de Vendôme appointing Piaras Grás to his staff.

'What do you know of this?' he asked, flourishing it in my face. I made no reply but the Sieur had no doubts. 'French spies,' he said. 'Well, we have a short way with spies here. Take them out,' he ordered his men. 'You will find plenty of trees outside.'

I was dragged to my feet when there was an unexpected interruption. He strode to the door and there stood Aimée Neffer, looking lovelier than ever.

'Mademoiselle Neffer,' he began, 'you have come at an inopportune moment.' Then he noticed that she was staring at us. 'Do you know these prisoners?'

'Who would know them better,' she said venomously. 'They are my father's bitterest enemies.'

'Then you are in time to be avenged. We are going

to hang them.'

'No,' she cried. 'Let us do it a better way. Deliver these spies to our prince. That way I will be revenged, for he will hang them and,' she smiled coquettishly at him, 'you will receive a rich reward.'

I could hardly believe my ears, but it seemed plain that Muiris had been right and that Aimée Neffer had made a fool of me. The only puzzling thing was that she had not mentioned anything of the story I had told her. I gazed at her coldly and I fancied a momentary sadness crossed her face, but she gave the Sieur her hand to kiss and went away saying, 'Adieu until tomorrow.'

The Sieur was well pleased with her suggestion. He ordered his men to take us to the château and lock us in the dungeons. We were dragged up a steep, rugged pathway until we stood before the grim castle. Heavy gates opened and clanged behind us; then we were dragged along stone passages and down steps into a cell. Still bound we were thrown to the floor and bolts were shot into place.

'Muiris,' I said, 'I'm afraid I've brought bad luck to you.'

'I knew the risks before we set out,' he replied, 'but I'm afraid the mademoiselle was only playing with us the whole time.'

I was silent. Her actions puzzled me. If it were not for her our dead bodies would now be swinging from some tall pine. Muiris's heavy breathing told me he had fallen asleep. My own eyes began to grow heavy. Hope seemed very far away, and I too fell asleep pondering.

EIGHTEEN

Aimée Comes

It must have been several hours later that I was awakened by something running across my face. With a loud cry I tried to spring to my feet but fell back heavily. The cell was as black as night, but I could hear scrabbling and with horror I realised that we were surrounded by rats.

'Muiris! Muiris!' I shouted. 'Wake up. We must free ourselves. The place is swarming with rats.'

'What can we do?' he asked.

I hardly knew, but anything was better than lying there at the mercy of these horrible creatures. By rolling over I got close to where Muiris lay and I found his hands. I bent my head and grawed and bit at the cords which bound them. My teeth ached and my lips bled, but I kept on working until at last I felt a knot loosen. A few minutes more and I had freed his hands, which fell numb and useless to his sides.

Gradually the blood flowed back and he worked at my bonds until they fell away and at least we were able to drive off the rats. A couple of hours passed and we tried to keep up our spirits with various little devices but the damp dark cell was a dreary place. Suddenly we heard footsteps in the passage outside. The bolts were drawn back, the door swung inwards and our eyes were dazzled for a moment by the light of a lantern. We saw with astonishment that our visitor was Aimée Neffer.

I received her coldly. 'You played your game well, Mademoiselle.'

She looked at me uncomprehendingly. 'What do you mean?' she asked. 'Surely you do not doubt me? I have worked only to save you. I pretended to be your enemy, but only that I might help you, and I have coquetted with a man I loathe just to serve you.'

I was still unconvinced. 'How can we trust you after last night?'

'How can you doubt me?' she retorted. 'If I had not persuaded the Sieur of my enmity you would not be here now.'

That was certainly true for we would have been hanged, but I was proud and did not want to admit yet that I had been wrong.

'I have brought you some food,' she went on. 'It was the best I could get and you had better eat it so that you will be strong enough for what we must do in a few hours' time.'

She stretched out her hand to me. 'What have I to gain by coming here?' she asked. 'If the Sieur suspected he would not spare me, even though he is in love with me.'

I was filled with shame and self-reproach. 'Mademoiselle,' I began, 'I am a miserable wretch. I have been mad, ungrateful. . .' but she stopped me.

'We are friends again,' she said, and turning to Ó Briain she asked, 'What do you say, Monsieur?'

'I doubted you, Mademoiselle,' he said simply, 'but now I trust you in everything.'

'Now listen,' she said. 'The Sieur trusts me because

I have promised to be his wife. I have deceived him, I'm afraid, but it was for you. He has sent word to the Prince of your capture, so we must make our escape tonight. He believes you safe here so there is no guard. I will come back later and we will try to make our way out. It is a plan full of dangers, but there is no other way out. And now,' she said, 'I must go,' and taking the lantern she left us, two men overwhelmed with gratitude and remorse.

NINETEEN

Freedom—The Flight across the Mountains

The hours crawled by. The fetid dungeon with its slimy walls and swarming vermin had seemed bad enough before. Now in the light of new hope it was unbearable. What if Aimée should fail? What if the Sieur's suspicions were aroused? I tortured myself with such thoughts and was about to utter them to Muiris when a light step sounded, hurrying along th the passage.

The shaft of light through the grating in the door grew larger and the bolts were drawn back. As Aimée came through the door we uttered a low cry of welcome.

'Hush,' she whispered. 'I'm afraid the Sieur suspects something. I could hardly get away.' She thrust two stout hunting knives into our hands. 'These were the only weapons I could get.'

Suddenly we heard heavy footsteps coming along the passage. 'Whoever it is,' whispered Aimée, 'you must overpower him, otherwise he will raise the alarm.'

The steps came closer and it seemed an age until they stopped outside. Then Aimée gasped in horror, 'The Sieur must have followed me.'

As the door swung inward we crouched behind it hidden from his view. Then with sudden spring I was on him, gripping his throat. He struggled like a madman but I choked him into silence. I stripped off his coat and boots and took his pistols; then we thrust a gag into his mouth and tied him up with our own bonds. A look of such hatred distorted his features that Aimée shuddered.

'Come,' she whispered. 'I am afraid.'

We left him in the darkness bolting the door behind us and Aimée led the way along the passage and up the flight of stone steps where she extinguished the lantern.

'We must go on in the darkness,' she breathed. 'Be careful. A sound would betray us.'

We peered out into the passage ahead of us and saw one of the Sieur's men coming towards us. As he reached us I struck him with the haft of my knife. He slumped to the ground and we quickly took his clothes and helmet for Muiris. Through the long passages we sped and at length came out into the open air where the most dangerous part of our attempt lay, for now we had to pass the guards.

Aimée took my arm as the Sieur's fiancée and with Muiris following we made our way to the gate.

In a hoarse voice I ordered one of the guards to open
up and we strolled through in a leisurely fashion. We
longed to run as we got outside but we had to
pretend that we had all the time in the world.

When we felt that we were out of sight we halted
with one accord to enjoy the beauty of the night and
the sweet air of freedom. Then we hastened on,
through gorse and rocks, into streams and over
quagmires, scarcely pausing to breathe and fearing all
the time to hear the alarm bell. To Muiris and me in
stout boots the journey was painful, but to Aimée
the sharp stones and icy streams must have been
misery. But she carried on undaunted, leading us
through paths known only to experienced mountaineers like herself.

At last I stopped and said, 'Mademoiselle, you
must not walk any further. Muiris and I will take
turns to carry you.'

She protested but we persuaded her that we could
make better speed and thus we continued for another
hour. The way was becoming steeper and more
difficult and feeling that we could safely halt before
attempting the worst of it, we sat down on a bank of
ferns and took a brief rest.

TWENTY

Pursuit—Defeat in Victory

As we took our rest we tried to tell ourselves that we were safe; that the Sieur had not yet been rescued; or that if he had our enemies had missed us in their pursuit. Then a shot rang out. It might have been a solitary hunter, but we dared not take that chance. We rose and continued our weary journey. We were carrying Aimée now on a sling improvised from a couple of saplings and our cloaks, and elevated on our shoulders she could keep a sharp watch.

We were getting along rapidly when suddenly she cried out, 'we are being pursued.'

Looking back we saw about a dozen men fanned out on the side of the mountain above us.

'*M'anam do Dhia!*' cried Muiris. 'Look front.'

Some distance in front on our left there was a second party. We were out of range of their fire, but they would be able to make quicker progress than we could.

'If only we could reach shelter,' I said. 'On this plain. . .'

'About half a mile ahead,' said Aimée, 'there is a chasm crossed by a little wooden bridge. If we could only reach it. . .'

'On, on,' I cried and we dashed forward swinging Aimée from side to side as we sped. The going was rough; behind us the yells of our enemies came closer and closer; in front, a few yards away, lay safety.

At last we reached it and were hidden for a moment by the rough terrain. 'Cross the bridge with Mademoiselle, Muiris,' I panted, 'and see if it can be broken down. When you are ready a whistle will warn me. If I do not come in fifteen minutes, destroy the bridge and go on.'

They both protested but I was giving the orders.

I hid behind a huge boulder and waited for our enemies to come. If I could keep them back until Muiris had crossed the bridge we had a chance. I waited until they were within pistol shot and fired. There was a loud cry and I could hear the Sieur tell his men to move cautiously. Keeping out of sight I ran to another boulder and fired again. Would the whistle never come? If the Sieur should guess there was but one man! I had one shot left when shrilling through the night air came a long drawn out whistle. I raced to the bridge, shots whistling over my head as I sped to where Muiris was hacking at the lashings. We cut and slashed and then with a grinding crash it toppled into the gorge below.

I saw the Sieur turn and give an order.

'Down,' I shouted, pulling Aimée to the ground as a volley rang out. I heard a sharp sound from Muiris and as we were about to move on he staggered and all but fell.

'What has happened?' I cried.

'Piaras,' he said, 'my time has come.' He had been fatally hit. 'You remember that day we talked in the hospital? I had a feeling then that my time was near.'

I was overcome with anguish at the thought of

losing my loyal friend and Aimée could not speak for tears. His mind wandered a little and he spoke of old friends and his native Clare. Then with scarcely a tremor the gallant soldier passed away as we knelt beside him.

We covered him with branches and piled stones about him. Then with heavy hearts we journeyed on.

TWENTY-ONE

Refuge—A Debt Well Paid

It was almost dawn when we reached Gaspard's cottage. He welcomed us and gave us some food while Aimée related all that had happened. I urged Aimée then to go into the inner room and rest a little and she agreed, but warned Gaspard to keep guard outside. 'This place is far from the château, but the Sieur is revengeful and might follow us.'

I sat alone in front of the log fire thinking of poor dead Muiris and the Duc's mad scheme to seize the Sieur. What could I do now single-handed? I might as well return and hand up my sword and life to the Duc. Thus brooding I fell asleep.

I was awakened by the sound of a struggle and leapt to my feet as the door was hurled inward. There, covered with mud, dishevelled and with bloodshot eyes stood the Sieur. With a heavy blow he felled me and burst into the room where Aimée lay sleeping.

'Jade,' he shouted, 'this is for your treachery,' and there followed the crack of a pistol and a cry.

I sprang upon him and we grappled for each other's throats. All my passions were let loose as I thought of Muiris and that gentle girl. Gradually I felt him weaken before my ferocious assault and raising him I hurled him against the wall. With a crash he fell to the floor and lay still.

I rushed in to find Aimée covered in blood. Aghast I fell to my knees beside her and cursed myself that she had been brought to this through helping me.

'I am happy that I have been able to repay the great debt I owed you,' she said faintly.

'Aimée,' I said, anguished, 'can you forgive me for thinking you capable of betraying me?'

'We women forgive everything to those we love,' she said softly.

There was a sound outside and Gaspard came in, white and haggard. He gazed at Aimée, transfixed with horror.

'Gaspard,' she whispered, 'go to my father and tell him all.' Then to me, 'raise me up, Piaras. The time is here.' I lifted her gently and her dark head sank against my shoulder; with a little sigh she was gone.

'Who did this?' said Gaspard hoarsely.

'The Sieur,' I answered.

He raised his knife and rushed to where the Sieur lay, still unconscious, but I stopped him. 'He is my prisoner. You will be avenged.'

He told me then how the Sieur and two followers had crept up on him. He had killed both but the Sieur had struck him down. We bound the unconscious prisoner and Gaspard left to bring Henri Neffer.

Night fell and still they had not returned. I was

waiting outside the cottage when I heard something and turning saw the Sieur, who had somehow freed himself, running to safety. I raced after him as he laughed mockingly; then a shot rang out and I saw him throw up his arms and stagger, as a small body of men led by Gaspard, came into view. Gaspard had killed the Sieur and my mission was ended. But at what cost!

I told the whole story to Henri Neffer who gazed grief-stricken at the lovely face of his dead daughter.

'I have often fought the French,' he said, 'but for your conduct towards my daughter I offer you my hand in friendship.' And we shook hands, the Franco-Irish officer and the Vaudois chief, as his men lifted their sad burden.

Bareheaded I accompanied the little procession for a few miles and then watched as the mountain peaks hid it from view. Then with deep sadness I turned my face towards Ivrea.

TWENTY-TWO

Again at Ivrea

Reveille was sounding through the camp as I made my way to the quarters of the Duc de Vendôme. I had won back my former place but I felt that it had been at far too great a cost.

The Duc came in shortly and I saluted, waiting for him to speak.

'M. de Grás,' he said coolly. 'You have come back. I thought you had failed.'

'I have succeeded, Milord,' I said bitterly, 'but at too high a price. The Sieur will trouble you no more, but my two friends lie in their graves.'

He looked searchingly at me. 'Of whom do you speak?' he inquired.

'Of Lieutenant Muiris Ó Briain, who accompanied me, and of a gentle mountain girl,' I answered.

He was silent for a little. Then he said, 'I understand, M. de Grás, but I too had a friend to whom your sword gave death. Where does Ó Briain lie?'

'Far up the mountain by La Gorge,' I told him.

'Can you guide a party to the place?' he queried.

I nodded silently.

'I will send for him. Now go. But remember, if you have your memories, so have I.'

I saluted and left, but felt I had come to understand him better. He was a man who had himself felt deep friendship so he could understand my grief. And he could honour the bravery of one of his soldiers. I recognised now the qualities which had earned the Duc the loyalty of his men.

Several hours later I set out with a party up the mountain. We lifted poor Muiris from his lonely grave and brought him down to his final resting place amid the men of his own regiment.

TWENTY-THREE

Despondency—Sheldon's Again—
The Call to Ireland

The Duc's campaign continued successfully and Ivrea and Verrua yielded to our arms. I was still attached to his staff and went about my duties in a routine way. All enthusiasm and ambition seemed to have left me as the shadow of the recent sad events hung over me still.

Some time after the surrender of Verrua the Duc sent for me and told me that he had decided to transfer me back to my former regiment. I could have thrown my cap in the air for joy but that would have been unsoldierly conduct before the Maréchal.

'Monsieur de Nugent wants to bring his numbers up to full strength,' he said. 'I have written to him mentioning your service here and suggesting that you be promoted to a captaincy. I feel I have done you an injury and I owe it to you to say that I now believe that you were blameless in the matter of the Chevalier de Frobin.

I could hardly speak for amazement. I was elated by my transfer, but to be recommended for promotion by the Duc and to hear him apologise to a mere lieutenant astounded me. I stumbled out my thanks to this strange man and left.

Within a few weeks I was back among my old comrades of Sheldon's who were now fighting in

Flanders. With them I shared many glories and many losses including the disaster of Ramillies. On that dreadful day we fought beside our countrymen of Clare's Regiment while our commanding officer, the Duc de Villeroi, so mishandled the battle that it turned into a rout. Our losses were so great that for many months our squadrons could not take the field.

It had not occured to me that our losses would affect my future, but fate holds many surprises in store. One day our colonel sent for me. He was with other Brigade officers and he came to the point at once.

'Captain Grás,' he said, 'our regiments have suffered heavy losses and we consider it necessary to recruit in Ireland. This is a dangerous service requiring great secrecy and I have thought of you for it. Would you consider it? Think carefully before you answer.'

It did not take me long to decide. 'When do I start?' I asked.

'Good man,' said Colonel Nugent. 'You sail from Dunkirk in a few weeks. You will have to work as circumstances dictate, but be careful and watchful. Remember what success will mean to the Brigade.'

I saluted and hurried away, overjoyed at the chance to see my homeland again even though it would be as a stranger and an outlaw.

TWENTY-FOUR

A Gentleman of Leisure in Dublin

'Help! Help, sir!'

A girlish voice sounded in the darkness as I made my way to Tom's Coffee House which stood near Dublin Castle. Quickly I swung round on my heel but could see nothing for a few seconds. Then in the murky light of an oil lamp I saw several struggling figures beside a sedan-chair. With a warning shout I dashed forward drawing my sword and three or four figures fled down a laneway.

Sword in hand I went towards the sedan-chair and bowing to the occupant said, 'Madame, I trust you are not hurt.'

'No, sir,' she said, 'but what might have happened but for your assistance. The streets are so unsafe at night.'

'The unsafe streets have done me a service,' I replied gallantly. 'May I escort you home?'

She gratefully accepted and the bearers, nothing worse for the fracas, lifted the chair while I fell in beside it. I did not wish to intrude by talking but she called me over and told me that she had been to a concert and was going home when her chair was set upon by four ruffians whom my timely interference had put to flight.

We wended our way beneath swinging signs and smoky oil lamps through Winetavern Street and so along to Usher's Quay where the bearers halted. I assisted the unknown young lady from the chair and accompanied her to the steps of a tall house. She thanked me graciously for my kindness and hoped that we might meet again.

I stood looking after her graceful figure as it vanished through the doorway of the fine house and then, with a sigh, retraced my steps towards Tom's Coffee House. It was useless for me to indulge in thoughts of fair young ladies. My days were spent either in warfare or, as now, in a secret struggle against the very Ascendancy of which this charming girl was undoubtedly a member. If she knew the purpose of my presence in Dublin she would, surely, hand me over to the law.

And so I made my way back through the crowded, noisy streets to the Coffee House and was soon engaged in a dicing game with one of the officers who frequented it. I was known to these as Ebenezer Swetenhall, gentleman, who had once served in the army of Her Majesty Queen Anne and who drank readily to the new dynasty and the confusion of the Jacobites. Meanwhile I kept my ears open for whatever information came my way.

Tonight, however, I had no interest in the game, and after a while I threw down my dicebox, bade my opponent, one Captain Wildair of the Queen's Dragoons, good night and walked back to my lodgings in the Corn Market. Soon afterwards I was sound asleep and dreaming of a fair young lady whose name I did not even know.

TWENTY-FIVE

A Whisper from the Past

I had been in Dublin for several weeks carrying out my commission of recruiting for the ranks of the Brigade. Outwardly I was a gentleman with money and leisure to spend in taverns and wherever the members of fashionable society disported themselves. I had come to know many of them, so that I had entrée to some of the best houses in the metropolis.

But all the time I was moving among the people and many a silver coin passed from my hand to that of some youngster burning to shoulder a musket in the Brigade. It was a dangerous existence for if my Ascendancy friends knew of my double life they would make short work of me.

So from day to day the work went on but never since our first meeting did I catch a glimpse of the lady whose face haunted me. Sometimes I found myself straying near to the stately house on Usher's Quay and I would tell myself sternly that I must put such foolishness out of my mind. Indeed I tried to, and I had flattered myself into the belief that I had succeeded when we met again.

I was strolling with two officers on the Mall one evening when a sedan-chair stopped and a young lady descended. By accident or design she dropped her fan and I stepped quickly forward to pick it up. As I handed it to her our eyes met and looking directly at me she asked if we had not met before.

I reminded her of the occasion and she smiled. 'Ah yes,' she said, 'and I do not even know the name of my preserver.'

'Captain Ebenezer Swetenhall, very much at your service,' I bowed.

'I have heard of you, Captain,' she said winningly. 'Will you be at Lady Brudenel's ball on Thursday? Mary Sickles would like to repay her obligation.'

Sickles! Surely she could not be connected with my old enemy! The memory of that unfortunate night in Cathair Domnhaill five years ago flashed into my mind, but I thrust it aside because I did not want to link her with it. Raising to my lips the hand she offered me I murmured that I hoped to see her then, and we parted.

* * * * *

On Thursday I made sure to be mingling with the elite at Lady Brudenel's elegant mansion. I studied the brilliant throng but could see no sign of my charming acquaintance when her well-known voice sounded from behind me.

We danced a minuet and I feasted my eyes on her beauty. She was dressed in a cream-coloured gown which floated about her in graceful folds, her glorious auburn hair was dressed high and she had a dreamy look in her brown eyes. When the dance was over we moved to a quiet alcove where she sat and chatted to me for a little while. I gave myself up to the full enjoyment of the occasion because within a few weeks

my work would take me away from Dublin and I
would pass out of her life for ever. At length she had
to go, and as I watched her during the rest of the
evening my admiration and worship deepened with
every minute.

At the end of the evening I went to bid her adieu,
and as I made my way down the crowded staircase I
was brought back from my dreamings to work as the
voice of one of the finely dressed dandies whispered
in my ear: 'Tomorrow evening at seven. By the seashore at Bullock. Everything is ready.'

TWENTY-SIX

By Bullock Strand—A Loyalist Volunteer

The next evening under a starlit sky I turned my
horse towards Bullock to supervise the embarkation.
As I rode along by the lonely shore, my face hidden
under a velvet mask, the mournful cry of a curlew
came to my ears like some warning of danger, but I
paid little heed to it. My plans were well laid.

In twos and threes the young recruits made their
way to the rendezvous and I shook their hands as
they took their places in the boat to be rowed to
where the smuggler ship waited, her sails set. The
embarkation completed, the muffled oars fell into the
rowlocks and with a quick handclasp the captain took
his place.

I stood on the shore watching them pull away and
heard no other sound until a voice rang out, 'Stand in

the Queen's name.' A couple of shots rang out and I heard the tramp of feet not fifty yards away. Cocking my pistols I fired in the direction of the sound and leaping on my horse spurred away as shots followed me.

Making a detour I rode rapidly towards the city and reached my lodgings safely. I changed my clothes and sauntered down to Tom's Coffee House for a game of cards.

Some two hours later an officer came in spattered with mud. He was a Lieutenant Jones and I observed that he seemed to have had a rough time.

'Some damned traitor was sending off recruits to France,' he growled, and described the incident at Bullock.

'I daresay you would know him again,' I suggested.

'You're wrong there,' he said. 'We could see him plainly but his face was masked. I'll catch him yet, and see that he hangs.'

We all heartily echoed this sentiment and began to discuss ways and means of capturing this ruffian. I suggested that we form ourselves into a volunteer group who would help the military to patrol the roads and keep a special eye on Bullock. The scheme was warmly approved and various loyal gentlemen offered their services. When I proposed that we appoint a captain I was immediately chosen as being the liveliest of the group. I thanked my friends for the honour and our party broke up.

I returned to my lodgings. There I slipped a pair of loaded pistols into my pocket and wrapping a long dark cloak about me I went out again. A few minutes' walk brought me to Fishamble Street where I went through an archway and knocked on a door. A whispered word let me in and I went down a long narrow passage into a room lit by one candle. Two men were seated before a blazing fire, one of them Charles Jans, the dandy who had spoken to me at Lady Brudenel's party.

I related the events of the evening, my narrow shave and my later appointment as captain to the new volunteer group. As such I would be free to go everywhere and speak to anyone, even those suspected of recruiting or smuggling, for it would be in the course of my duty. We agreed that we must find another embarkation point, while I would direct my volunteer patrol to Bullock.

It was after midnight when we parted, and as I turned into Fishamble Street I almost collided with Lieutenant Jones.

'A late hour and a strange place, Captain,' he said curiously.

I shrugged off the comment and said good night but I had the feeling that his interest in me boded no good.

TWENTY-SEVEN

Love is not for Me—
Checkmate to an Enemy

I had one more day in Dublin. The last draft of my recruits would sail from Howth the next evening and then I would head for my native south. I felt a sense of relief. Since that meeting with Jones in Fishamble Street I had had a notion that I was being watched and whenever we met I felt his beady eye fixed on me suspiciously. Outwardly my standing with my associates appeared to be unaffected and that night I was due to attend a ball. I wondered if I would have the good fortune to meet Mistress Sickles whom I had not seen since the evening in Lady Brudenel's.

Dressed in elegant style I joined the fashionable throng in the great house and was soon laughing and chatting gaily with them. At the same time I managed to slip a note to my fellow conspirator Charles Jans telling him that I would be guiding my volunteer troop to Bullock the following evening, thus clearing the way for him to carry out the embarkation at Howth.

Then I went in search of the girl who still filled my thoughts. I found her surrounded by a circle of young men but she rose at once as I entered and came over to me. We moved away together and I fought back an overwhelming desire to tell her of my love. What right had I to entangle her free and happy existence with my dangerous lot? But I could not refrain from telling her that I was going away and to my great delight I saw that she was really sorry.

'I had hoped our acquaintance would be of longer duration,' she said, 'but I shall never forget the service you did me.'

We had one joyous last dance together. Then other partners came to claim her; and I had to finish the business I had come to do.

For this purpose I made my way to the card room. As I approached I heard the unmistakeable voice of Lieutenant Jones saying, 'Who is he? Where did he come from? What if he should be a Jacobite spy?'

Silence fell as I walked in and it was clear that he had been speaking of me.

'May I inquire,' I asked the room in general, 'in what way my actions interest you, gentlemen?'

Once again it was Jones who spoke. 'We think you keep strange company,' he asnwered, 'and that you often ride in the direction of Bullock which has no very loyal reputation.'

'The sea air is pleasant there, gentlemen,' I said to the company again, ignoring Jones. 'The scenery is pretty and there is information to be picked up.'

There was a murmur of agreement at this so I drove home my advantage.

'I would be very careful using words like Jacobite spy. They have an ugly sound. If Lieutenant Jones must see a Jacobite spy in every honest gentleman who comes amongst you I am truly sorry. As for Bullock, you, my friends, shall ride there with me tomorrow evening.' And I went on to explain that I had picked up a rumour of a sailing from Bullock which I thought we ought to investigate.

The suggestion was received with enthusiasm and Lieutenant Jones's suspicions were forgotten, at least for the moment. What was more, I believed that I had succeeded in diverting attention away from Howth.

TWENTY-EIGHT

A Wild-Goose Chase—
A Little Swordplay

A lively party of us set out for Bullock on the following evening. The authorities had taken alarm and a troop of military under the command of Captain Wildair, my gambling partner of Tom's Coffee House, accompanied us. I rode along beside him chatting as we went.

As we drew near the seashore the order to dismount was given and we crept forward on foot. When we reached the beach all we could see was the full moon shining down on a placid sea and an empty strand. The only sound came from the ceaseless motion of the waves and the lonely call of the sea birds.

Turning to my companions who stood around, disappointment written on all their faces, I said, 'Gentlemen, our ride seems to have been for nothing. The rats have kept to their holes tonight.'

Dead silence greeted my remark and I felt that their suspicions had returned. Then a commotion began at the rear of the group and Lieutenant Jones pushed his way forward, quivering with rage.

'We have been brought on a wild-goose chase,' he cried furiously. 'It seems the Captain knows and hears tales which never reach the ears of others.'

'Comrades,' I said, 'we might have had better luck. But the lieutenant seems angry.'

'Yes,' shouted Jones, 'angry about you and your fine stories. What is known about you?'

'If the lieutenant does not know me to be a loyal gentleman,' I said, 'he is an ass.'

'I demand an apology,' cried Jones, drawing his sword.

Turning to Wildair I asked if he would act for me and in a few minutes all was arranged.

Our swords crossed on the beach under the light of the moon as around us stood a circle of the military and our volunteer group. It was over quickly. Jones was too angry to use any skill. I retreated before his wild onslaught and then slowly began to press him backwards. In his fury he constantly exposed himself to my blade and I pondered if I should kill him. But I was leaving Dublin on the following day and his suspicions and innuendoes could hardly matter to me any longer.

He made a fierce lunge at me which I parried and then my blade leaped out and passed through his left shoulder.

With a cry of pain he staggered back shouting, 'Swetenhall, beware! I'll meet you again.'

Perhaps for an instant I regretted that my thrust had not been lower, but I had won and that was all that mattered then.

TWENTY-NINE

An Old Friend

The long shadows of a June night had fallen across the land as I urged my tired horse along the rough road leading to Cathair Domnhaill. It was several days since I had left Dublin and galloped away to the heather-clad hills and wild glens of my youth. I knew that I would find many brave young men there eager to welcome the chance of taking their place in the Brigade. But the country was full of spies who would be happy to take the golden reward for uncovering a French recruiting officer, so I took care to avoid the larger towns and kept to the villages and hamlets along my route.

Now I was almost at my journey's end. As I reached the top of a steep incline I reined in my horse and gazed down on the dear old place I had left as a fugitive five years before. I wondered if Sir Michael Sickles had recovered from the wound I had given him; and if I would meet brave old Mícheál Mór who had saved me from the consequences of my deed. Would he know me? It would be hard to recognise in the tall, broad-shouldered Captain Hall (for I had left Captain Swetenhall behind me along the road) the stripling who had fled the country on that stormy night.

I moved on and my horse, knowing that he would soon be resting for the night, galloped the last few yards and brought me to the door of the inn.

I dismounted and as I stepped across the threshold I saw my old friend Mícheál who, as landlord, came forward to meet me. I asked for a meal and lodgings for the night. After I had eaten I sent for Mícheál to bring me to my room. He came immediately and as we went upstairs I asked if I might have a private word with him inside. He entered rather cautiously and set the candle on the table as I closed the door.

'Do you remember a young fellow who broke the law and fled to France one night about five years ago?' I asked him.

He was instantly wary. 'I know little of such things,' he said.

'I was told it was an innkeeper who helped him,' I went on.

'I seldom hear what is going on,' he said again. 'The inn keeps me busy.'

But I could keep up the pretence no longer and removing my hat and the black beard I had now adopted I said, 'Mícheál, it is Piaras Grás who stands before you.'

He was astonished and delighted, but then alarmed. 'I never hoped to see you again,' he said, 'but why have you come here and in this way?'

I told him of my work for the Brigade and regaled him with some of my adventures. But he warned me again of danger. 'I will keep your secret,' he said, 'but the whole country is full of spies.'

As he turned to go I said, 'Remember, Mícheál, your new guest is a Captain Hall, an English gentleman, travelling for pleasure.'

With a loud 'Good night, Captain,' he left and in a few minutes I was fast asleep after my long days of travel.

THIRTY

Love whispers again—An Invitation

For some days I rested very quietly at the inn and then began in earnest my work of recruitment. Day and night I was on the go, in this hamlet and that town, up in the mountains and down in the deep glens. I attended wakes and funerals and wherever the people gathered, and received the fealty of many a fine young stalwart under the shadow of Carrantuohill or while the moonlight danced on the waters of Lough Currane.

And at night little vessels would creep out of some lonely cove carrying their cargo of 'wild geese' just as I had slipped away across the kindly sea five years ago.

One day I had been out since early morning amongst the people whose dwellings lay around my old home. I had got word that there would be a gathering at a funeral and I knew well that I should reap a rich harvest of recruits from among their number. When my work was done I turned back towards the inn but the mellow beauty of the summer evening brought thoughts of my happy childhood and I felt an unconquerable longing to see the old place again. Almost unconsciously I turned in that direction.

A ride of a few miles brought me within view of it. There it stood, calm and majestic, its grey, ivy-covered walls lit by the setting sun. I fought off the bitter memories. To what purpose were my vain regrets? But as I rode away the road took me past the little cottage where my father had spent his last days. Nothing remained of it but roofless walls, and as I gazed grief-stricken at the ruins, seeing the final uprooting of the Gráses, I was recalled sharply to the present by the sound of horses.

A group of riders trotted by and with a sudden, fierce throb I recognised the rich auburn hair and graceful figure of my dream girl. I resisted the mad impulse to ride after her, for surely by now I was long forgotten. Her charming behaviour had simply been good manners and gratitude for a service rendered. My profession was soldiering and I would think only of that. But once again I had reckoned without fate.

*   *   *   *   *

For some time after that I continued quietly with my work. The people kept my secret and the law appeared unaware of my existence. And then one day I was startled out of the even tenor of my ways.

I was eating in the dining-room of the inn when I heard a heavy step and Sir Michael Sickles, of all people, burly and red-faced as ever came in. Mícheál brought the wine he had ordered and flashing me a warning glance asked, 'Can I do anything more for you, Captain?'

I shook my head and went on with my meal in silence. After a time Sir Michael spoke, asking me a few general questions about my travels. Then he said, 'You are a military man, I gather, and I know all you officers enjoy a game of cards. You must come and visit me at Snaidhm Castle.'

Here was a dilemma: invited to my old home by the man who had usurped it; against whom I had turned my pistol; who accepted me as an English officer when in fact I was recruiting for the Brigade. Could I accept? But dare I refuse? There was some danger in acceptance but on the other hand to refuse him might arouse his enmity. He might start to make inquiries about the English military man who was strangely unwilling to visit people of his own kind and that would be most undesirable in the circumstances. While if my visit were successful, it would give me a kind of official sanction which might turn to be very useful.

And so, with an airy politeness I was far from feeling, I accepted. He shook hands vigorously and left, telling me that he would expect me the following evening.

When he had gone I sat cursing the unhappy chance which had brought us together again. I thought of not turning up at the castle, but I knew that would only make things worse. When I told Mícheál about it he shook his head in dismay. 'God grant nothing evil comes out of it,' he said.

THIRTY-ONE

The Daughter of an Enemy

It was with very mixed feelings that I presented myself at Snaidhm Castle the following evening. I felt extremely bitter as I followed the servant through the spacious, well-remembered hall but knew that I must suppress all outward signs of emotion.

My host was too stolid to notice my perturbation and gradually I recovered my self-possession and talked to him of the gay life of Dublin—a safe subject since he seldom visited it. At last dinner was announced and I almost lost my self-control again as a girl came towards us and Sir Michael introduced her as his daughter.

I recovered myself and bowed over her hand, but my brain was in a whirl as I sat down. It was as I had already half-suspected and deeply feared. Mary Sickles was the daughter of my enemy. How I wished that I had never discovered the truth. Then at least I could have gone on dreaming of her.

Somehow the meal ended. Sir Michael who had eaten well went to sleep in his armchair and the conversation was left to Mary and myself. As we chatted I noticed that she looked thoughtfully at me every now and then but I sat on as if I had never partnered her in a dance or heard her voice before.

Suddenly she asked me if, during my time in Dublin, I had ever met a gentleman named Swetenhall.

I pondered but could not recall. 'What was he like?' I asked her, feeling like a criminal.

'Tall, handsome and dark-complexioned,' she replied. 'He did me a great service once.'

'I meet so many men in my wanderings,' I said. 'I cannot remember.'

She seemed disappointed but did not refer to the subject again and soon afterwards I left. My last memory of her was standing in the doorway as I departed, a soft breeze ruffling her hair.

I avoided Snaidhm Castle after that and took care never to be at home when Sir Michael called, as he did several times, at the inn.

Some weeks later, as I was strolling through a wood one evening, I heard the sound of a horse coming up behind me. I stepped aside to give it room to pass but the horse stopped beside me and a well-known voice spoke my name. For a moment I was confused, then I bowed and stood silently before Mary Sickles. She asked me to help her dismount as it was easier to talk when walking. I did so and we walked along in silence for a few moments when at last she said, 'Captain, you have not visited us lately. Did you not enjoy your visit, or is there some other reason why you have not come again?'

'Believe me, Mistress Sickles,' I said earnestly, 'there are reasons. I regret them for your sake as well as my own.'

'Surely you will allow us to brighten your stay among us?' she urged.

'If you knew whom you are inviting you would hardly press me,' I said, but I could not bring myself to tell her of the position between her father and myself.

'Come now, Captain,' she said laughing. 'You are trying to frighten me but you are making me all the more eager. You will come, Captain Hall; promise me.'

I could have fought anyone but her. With something very like a groan I consented. Then I assisted her to mount again and we parted.

THIRTY-TWO

For the Head of a Traitor— Love comes to Me

When I reached Snaidhm Castle the following evening I found Sir Michael reading an official looking document. He greeted me and then continued to read, but I was well content for Mary had just come in looking bewitching in a white dress.

'Gad, Hall,' he burst out suddenly. 'Here's a fine business. Some rebel of a Jacobite down here recruiting for the Frenchies. There, read that,' and he thrust the document at me.

It offered the reward of £500 for the capture of a French officer who was known to be recruiting in Kerry.

'What do you think of that, Hall?' he asked eagerly. 'A Jacobite spy among us. But I'll lay him by the heels.'

'I'm sure you will, Sir Michael,' I replied drily. 'No

one could doubt your zeal and activity.'

Was it fancy or did something flash into Mary's eyes?

Dinner was announced and Jacobite spies were temporarily forgotten as Sir Michael devoted himself to the pleasures of food and drink. After dinner Mary excused herself and I sat on with Sir Michael who soon fell asleep. I strolled out into the scented night and wandered through the garden. Presently there was a rustle beside me and a soft voice said, 'A penny for your thoughts, Captain Hall.'

'You shall have them, Mistress Sickles,' I said turning to her, 'but I warn you they are unpleasant enough.'

I had battled with myself all day and finally decided that I would tell her everything. I could not keep up the deception with this girl. She might bretray me, but I believed she would not.

'My thoughts,' I went on gravely, 'are those of a man who is playing a double part. I and the Captain Swetenhall you knew in Dublin are the same person.'

She looked steadily at me but said nothing.

'When your father gave me that document to read he little knew to whom he was showing it. I am the French officer who has been recruiting for the Brigade, but I am no spy. I serve my cause but I have never dishonoured it and I came here tonight to tell you, because it would be dishonourable to enter your father's house again.'

I paused, waiting for her reply. Looking me in the face she said, 'Though ten times £500 were on your head, and though I am Sir Michael Sickles's daughter, I will never betray you,' And she laid her hands in mine.

But I went on. 'There is something else, though it is a more painful secret.' I said, and I revealed to her the history of Snaidhm Castle and the dispossession of the Gráses.

'Why have you told me this tragic story?' she asked.

'Because I love you, have always loved you and because I cannot live a lie in your presence. But love is not for me, and so I ask that you will forgive the long deception, and let me carry your pardon into exile.'

'Why is love not for you?' she asked quietly. 'And what have I to forgive? It is you who have forgiven in loving me the daughter of your enemy. I have loved you since I first saw you in Dublin, Piaras.'

'But Mary,' I argued, 'I am an outlaw with a price on my head. I am an enemy to all you have been taught to hold dear.'

'What do I care if you are an outlaw?' she replied. 'I love you.'

For a few moments my work, my capture, Sir Michael, were all forgotten. And as I stooped to kiss her good night she whispered, 'Have faith in me. Your secret is safe.'

THIRTY-THREE

The Protection of the Law-Abiding

After that evening I kept far from the house which held my enemy and my love. Feverishly I pushed ahead with my task, facing constant danger and being often within an ace of capture.

Sometimes I drank wine with the officers of the military patrols who were out looking for me; at others I sent them off on long chases which would take them far from where I would be at my work. Everywhere I went little white proclamations offering reward for my capture fluttered in my face. And all the time Mary kept near to me. Whenever we could be together we would meet in the woods and wander away in happy forgetfulness.

One evening she came to me filled with anxiety and told me of a Lieutenant Jones who had arrived at the castle. From his conversation with her father she learned that he had been sent on special duty to hunt down the recruiting officer. She urged me to be extra vigilant and I assured her that I was not yet tired of life. But an error almost led to my undoing.

Perhaps I was careless but I enlisted a fellow who came to me by the wayside. As I gave him the silver something warned me not to trust him and I withheld the location of our rendezvous. A few days later as I stopped at an inn a group of troopers entered, among whom was my 'recruit' now in dragoon's uniform.

Pulling my hat over my eyes I lounged casually towards the door as a voice rang out, 'Stop him. It's the Jacobite spy.'

With a blow of my fist I levelled the nearest trooper and sprang on to my horse. The chase was furious and they began to gain on me. It was then I took a desperate decision. We were near Snaidhm Castle and urging my horse to his utmost speed I rode boldly in, giving my horse to a servant. Sir Michael was playing cards with Lieutenant Jones who did not recognise me and I watched the game for a while listening for the soldiers who were not long in coming.

As I heard them clatter in I removed my beard and told the men I was being pursued, but that if they continued with their game and said nothing all would be well. If they betrayed me, I said, my pistols were loaded and I would kill them.

They were filled with astonishment and fury but my pistols in their stomachs kept them silent. Sir Michael denied all knowledge of any French officer and when the leader of the troop pressed his inquiries he assumed a great show of indignation at the suggestion that such a scoundrel should be anywhere near his property.

When at last the troop departed I kept the two men seated until they should be well away from the area. When I judged it safe I insisted that they come to the door with me and remain while I mounted. As I bade them good night Lieutenant Jones snarled, 'I'll see you dancing at a rope's end yet.'

I laughed and rode away but had gone only a short distance when Mary called my name. She scolded me

for the risks I was taking and told me how she had
watched in terror as the troop rode off, certain that I
must be with them.

'Piaras,' she urged, 'when will this terrible danger
be at an end?'

'A few days more,' I told her, 'and then away to
merry France. But I have little to offer you in return
for your love and devotion. If you turn back now I
shall never blame you.'

'I love you, Piaras,' she said simply. 'I will follow
you to the ends of the earth.'

THIRTY-FOUR

The Frown of Fortune

But my charmed life could not last forever. I felt that
the coils were tightening but my work went on. I
enlisted recruits under the very noses of the
authorities, disguised as a parson here, a friar there;
today a gay dragoon, tomorrow a burly corn merchant.
I had left Mícheál's little inn for his safety, though he
had been upset at my going, and now slept wherever
chance offered. Then one day the blow fell.

With the recklessness born of constant danger I had
ridden out that morning without any disguise trusting
to my wits and the speed of my horse. I had been
going my way for several hours and had just parted
with a man who had brought me word of a gathering
in the mountains the following evening. Promising to

be there I turned to continue my way to the house of
a sympathiser when suddenly I heard the sounds of a
mounted patrol coming towards me. They were
hidden by a bend in the road and were close before I
became aware of them. As I turned my horse's head
a pistol shot rang out which frightened him. He
reared and threw me heavily, and as I rose to my feet
I saw Sir Michael Sickles and with him Lieutenant
Jones who shouted authoritatively, 'Surrender yourself in the Queen's name.'

For an instance I thought of resistance but there
were too many of them and I had no wish to die just
then. Sir Michael read ponderously from his official
document every word of which I knew, for it was
posted to every tree trunk in the country. He folded
the document as he finished and sneered, 'So we have
laid you by the heels at last.'

My sword and pistols were taken from me and,
mounted on my horse which one of the soldiers had
caught, I was led back to my old home Snaidhm
Castle. I was brought down a long corridor and into a
small room with barred windows. There they left me
tightly bound in a chair. As I heard the key grate in
the lock I felt I was indeed a prisoner. Underneath
the window a sentry's feet crunched up and down on
the gravel and there was a guard outside the door.

I knew that my stay would be a short one. I would
be sent next morning to some town to await trans-
portation to Dublin, and after that — the prospect
was grim but I could see little hope of escape. Several
times I thought of Mary who must know by now of
my capture but there was little she could do with

such a strict watch kept on me.

Uncomfortable though I was I must have fallen into a doze. Suddenly I awoke with the feeling that I was not alone. The sounds of the house had died away and even the monotonous step of the sentry outside the door seemed to have ceased. With a start I realised that someone was in the room; then a soft hand was laid over my mouth and a voice whispered, 'Hush. Do not make a sound.'

With eager hands Mary undid my bonds. I could not stand or move for a few minutes but after vigorous chafing the blood began to flow again. She led me out through the door which she locked carefully behind her. Stretched on the ground lay the sentry, breathing heavily.

'Drugged beer,' she murmured.

Noiselessly we moved down the corridor stopping only to return the key of my prison to Sir Michael's private room from which she had taken it earlier in the night. We stole past the dining room from which came the loud snores that told of Sir Michael and Jones sleeping off the celebration of my capture.

At last we were in the open air and then, after a farewell kiss, I sped away into the mountains to the cottage of a trusty friend.

THIRTY-FIVE

Consummation—Farewell

Five days had passed since my escape and I had not
been idle. Everything was ready for the completion
of my mission — and of my love story.

The word had gone round to my gallant recruits
and in the little creek where they were to rendezvous
the smuggler already lay waiting to spread her sails
and carry us swiftly to France. I had learned that *mo
chailín aluinn* would be at a ball held near her own
home that evening and my plans were all laid.

Before midnight I drew up my horse in a lonely
thicket beside the road she would travel homewards. I
was well screened from the view of anyone passing
by, but it was a long and lonely vigil. At last I heard
the distant rumble of a coach and prepared for action.

As the coach came into view I rode out from the
shadows and called a ringing 'Halt!' raising a pistol.
The coachman drew up at speed throwing his horses
back on their haunches and I ordered him and the
footman to throw away their arms which they
hurriedly did.

Sir Michael's head appeared through the window
demanding the reason for the stoppage.

'Sir Michael,' I said, 'I have come in fulfilment of a
duty. Your daughter has done me the honour of
giving me her love, and I have come to ask for her
here, where we are on more equal terms than at the

castle where you are surrounded by the instruments of your power.'

'Who are you,' he roared, 'who dares to stop a justice on the highway?'

'I am one you know well,' I replied calmly. 'I was recently your prisoner.'

'My daughter can have nothing to say to you, sir, an outlaw with a price on your head.'

'Let her speak for herself,' I answered as I dismounted, and opening the heavy door helped her to alight. As she did so she uttered a cry of warning and turning I saw the red-haired Jones rushing on me with drawn sword. Raising my pistol I fired and he staggered back, his sword arm hanging useless.

'That will be a warning, Lieutenant,' I said.

'Mistress Sickles,' I said, turning to Mary, 'you heard the proposal I have made to your father. I wish the time and place were more appropriate. We await your answer and I, at least, will abide by it.'

'Mary,' said Sir Michael, enraged, 'I forbid you to reply to this insulting footpad. Come; let us go and have done with this farce.'

She made no move to obey him, but placed her hand in mine. 'I love him, father,' she said simply.

'I forbid you to have anything to say to this spy, this low-bred scoundrel whom nobody knows,' he cried furiously.

'I am the son of the Grásach whose lands you hold,' I said proudly.

With a yell of rage he made to attack me but Mary placed herself between us.

'Father,' she said, 'I have obeyed you in everything,

but I cannot obey you in this. My heart is given.'

For a long time he stood silent. Then he said hoarsely. 'Go. Go with your outlaw. Go away out of my sight. You are no longer a daughter of mine.'

But she threw her arms around his neck. 'You will not send me away like this,' she said. 'Kiss me good-bye.'

And then this red-faced, loud-voiced usurper, a man whom I had despised, threw his arms around her and kissed her with convulsive affection. In that moment I found a new respect for him.

Then he turned to me. 'You have conquered,' he said. 'You have stolen my daughter. I had other aims for her than to marry an outlaw. Go. I cannot say more to my daughter's lover.'

With a new admiration I said to him, 'Sir Michael, your daughter is safe in my keeping.' Then lifting Mary on to my horse I sprang up behind her and we rode away. An hour later in a fisherman's cottage before a white-haired priest we said the words which made us man and wife.

The first faint light of dawn was breaking as our little ship spread her sails for the welcoming coast of France, her flight of 'wild geese' safely aboard.

As we stood looking back on the receding shores of the homeland I whispered to Mary, 'Have you any regrets?'

'Not while you are near, Piaras,' she murmured, and I bent and kissed her.

THE WILD ROSE OF LOUGH GILL

Patrick G. Smyth

Abridged by Maureen Donegan

The Wild Rose of Lough Gill, one of the most popular novels ever published in Ireland, is a colourful narrative written about the Confederate Wars. It is a fast-moving, romantic story of love and hate, war and kidnapping, cities besieged and gory battles with Cromwell stalking the land.

Edmund, the hero is involved in the Rebellion and his attempts to rescue Kathleen, the Wild Rose, from enemy hands is the central theme of the book. We see all the great historic events from their point of view and discover what effect the fall of governments, new laws and treaties had on their lives.

Seldom has a romance of such breathless excitement been combined with such a realistic picture of the times. This intriguing story ends shortly after the fall of Galway and the scene is set partly in Co. Sligo (near Lough Gill).